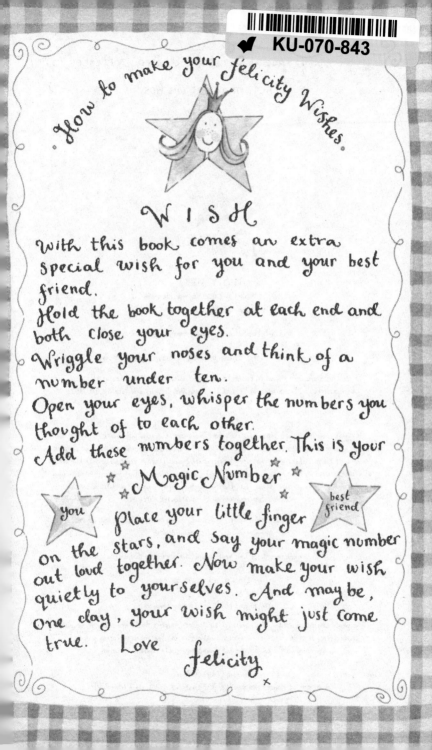

How to make your felicity Wishes

W I S H

With this book comes an extra special wish for you and your best friend.

Hold the book together at each end and both close your eyes.

Wriggle your noses and think of a number under ten.

Open your eyes, whisper the numbers you thought of to each other.

Add these numbers together. This is your

✶ Magic Number ✶

you

best friend

Place your little finger on the stars, and say your magic number out loud together. Now make your wish quietly to yourselves. And may be, one day, your wish might just come true.   Love

felicity

x

For my special penfriend Bea Forrester
with magical wishes
E.V.T

Emma Thomson's
felicity Wishes®

FELICITY WISHES
Felicity Wishes © 2000 Emma Thomson
Licensed by White Lion Publishing

Text and Illustrations © 2005 Emma Thomson

First published in Great Britain in 2005 by Hodder Children's Books

A Catalogue record for this book is available from the British Library

ISBN 0 340 90240 X

Printed and bound in China by Imago

The paper and board used in this paperback by Hodder Children's Books are natural recyclable
products made from wood grown in sustainable forests. The manufacturing processes
conform to the environmental regulations of the country of origin.

Hodder Children's Books
A division of Hodder Headline Ltd, 338 Euston Road, London NW1 3BH

CONTENTS

Perfect Penfriend

Felicity Wishes had spent hours hunting for her special pink pen but she still couldn't find it anywhere.

"Borrow mine," said Polly in a hushed voice as they were studying in the library.

"But it's not pink!" whispered Felicity.

"Does that matter?" asked Polly frowning.

Miss Page, the library monitor, glared in their direction and put her finger to her lips. "Shhhhhhh!"

"Yes it does matter," wrote Felicity on a scrap of paper and handed it to her friend.

"Why?" Polly scribbled back.

Felicity wiggled a beautiful sheet of sparkling pink paper in front of her friend's nose.

"I need to write a special letter," wrote Felicity, looking round to check that Miss Page wasn't watching them any more.

Polly suddenly stifled a squeal. Felicity's favourite pink pen was nestled neatly behind her ear! She tweaked it out and passed it to her friend, leaning over her shoulder to see who she was writing to.

Felicity was scribbling a response to an advert in Fairy Girl magazine. It read:

Being the friendliest fairy in Little Blossoming, Felicity had found Beatrice's appeal hard to ignore. By the end of lunchtime she'd written a four-page response telling Beatrice all about herself, her best friends, the School of Nine Wishes, and her favourite flavoured ice-cream.

"It's very good!" said Polly, after Felicity had shown the letter to her friends during break time.

"Are you sure it's OK?" asked Felicity. "You don't think it's too over the top?"

"No, honestly!" assured Holly. "It's wonderful!"

"I would love to get a letter from you," said Daisy. "Your letters are so magical."

Felicity skipped happily to the nearest postbox and made an extra-special wish just for Bea before posting her letter.

✳ ✳ ✳

Every day Felicity watched for the Post Fairy before she left for the School of Nine Wishes, and it wasn't long before a large yellow envelope landed on her doormat in a cloud of glitter.

"Isn't it great!" said Felicity excitedly to her friends when she finally arrived at school. "Bea's written four whole pages, on both sides too!"

Felicity's friends gathered round her, flapping their wings with excitement, as Felicity read out loud her very first penfriend letter.

"Gosh, it's so exotic!" said Holly admiring the beautiful paper. "They don't sell writing paper like this at the Fairy Stationers in Little Blossoming!"

"And her handwriting is so lovely! Do you think she writes like that naturally or do you think all fairies where she lives write like that?" pondered Polly.

"And look at the delicate flower she's attached to the letter. I've never seen anything as pretty as this ever. I wonder what it is?" asked Daisy.

Felicity picked up her fluffy pink pen straight away. "I'll write back to Bea and find out the answers to all your questions. I have a few questions myself – I want to know more about her friends, they sound so lovely!"

Over the next few weeks, Felicity and Bea exchanged letters almost every other day. Felicity couldn't believe they had so much in common!

Dear Beatrice

My best friend is Polly – she's good at everything and often has her head in the books, studying to be a tooth fairy. Then there are my other two friends, Holly and Daisy. You'd love them.

Holly is the queen of fashion in Little Blossoming and always looks stunning. Daisy is a real dreamer and loves spending time in her garden, chatting to her flowers. What are your friends like?

Write soon.
Love Felicity x

Self portrait

A few days later, Beatrice's reply dropped on Felicity's doormat. She flew downstairs as fast as her wings would take her and opened her letter straight away.

Dear Felicity,

Oh my goodness! Your friends sound fabulous and just like my friends! My best friend is Amber and she won first prize for the best smile competition this year. My other friend, Star, dreams of setting up her own fashion label one day, and Jasmine is green-fingered and works part-time at the local garden centre. I can't believe how similar they are!

Write soon.

Lots of love, Bea. xx

Me

13

After reading Bea's letter, Felicity suddenly had an idea! "Wouldn't it be wonderful if I met Bea, Polly met Amber, Daisy met Jasmine and Holly met Star!" she thought smiling to herself. "I am sure we would all get on really well and half-term is coming up so we could visit them then."

Quickly Felicity grabbed her pen and immediately set about writing back to Bea to share her big idea with her...

* * *

Holly, Polly and Daisy met for a milkshake at their favourite café, Sparkles. It seemed a bit too quiet without Felicity, who had been too busy writing to Bea to join them. The fairies had seen less and less of Felicity since she'd started writing to Bea. Whenever they did see her she was either poring over another letter from Bea or consumed with drafting her next letter. Holly, Polly and Daisy were beginning to feel a little left out.

Holly sighed and picked up a magazine and idly began to leaf through it.

"I've got it!" she said turning the magazine around to face the rest of her friends. "A holiday! Let's all go away together somewhere exciting where we can all have fun together just like we used to."

Daisy and Polly were delighted. It was a brilliant idea. Half-term was coming up and none of the fairies had gone away for ages, and they'd never been on holiday together before.

"Let's make it a surprise. Felicity loves surprises!" squealed Polly.

* * *

15

The fairy friends flew as quickly as they could down to the travel agent in Little Blossoming.

"There are so many places to choose from," said Polly, her nose pressed up against the travel agent's window. "How ever are we going to decide?"

There were activity holidays, relaxing holidays, sunshine holidays and snow holidays. The list was endless.

"Wow!" exclaimed Daisy. "We could go on a walking holiday to see species of flowers in their natural surroundings."

"Or we could go to Fairy Girl World to look at all the designer shops and sit in the cafés and watch out for famous fairies," suggested Holly, poring through a city-break leaflet.

"Let's try and find something that all of us will enjoy. Something with a little bit of everything," said Polly sensibly, making sure that her friends didn't get side-tracked by their own favourite activities.

After gathering up armfuls of catalogues, the three fairy friends headed home to draw up a shortlist of places to go. It was strange to be planning something so exciting without Felicity, but it would be even more exciting telling her when they'd booked it!

The next day at school break-time, Felicity was sitting in the library with her head buried in another glittery yellow envelope. Bea had thought Felicity's idea was fantastic so they were busy putting together the final touches to their surprise visit, making sure it all went to plan.

Suddenly, out the corner of her eye she saw Holly, Polly and Daisy giggling on the other side of the room. Felicity waved and mouthed a quiet 'hello'. But Holly, Polly and Daisy didn't see her.

"They look like they're having so much fun!" thought Felicity to herself. "I must meet up with them at lunch and find out what they've been doing. And I can tell them all about what Bea and I have been planning too!"

✳ ✳ ✳

But lunch-time came and went and by the time Felicity had flown to the Post

Office on Star Street and back to the
Large Oak Tree in the playing field
all her friends had gone. Finally, she
caught up with them at the end of
double-maths.

"I'd like to
invite you all
round to my
house for
tea on
Saturday,"
she said,
barely able
to hold in her excitement. "I haven't
seen you all in ages and we've got so
much to catch up on!!" she said with
a knowing smile.

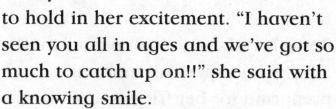

"That sounds great!" said Daisy
clapping her hands and winking at
the other fairies. It would be the
perfect opportunity to give Felicity
her surprise!

"I'll even make you one of my very

special chocolate cakes!" said Felicity excitedly.

"Oh," Holly, Polly and Daisy chorused, knowing that Felicity's cooking was normally a disaster!

"Do you mind if we bring our own cake?!" asked Daisy, trying not to hurt Felicity's feelings.

Felicity looked at Holly, Holly looked at Polly and Polly looked at Daisy. Suddenly, they couldn't control their giggles any longer and all burst out laughing.

✳ ✳ ✳

Saturday afternoon soon came and Felicity had spent all morning preparing for her friends' arrival. Every now and then she'd glance at Bea's latest letter propped up on the table and smile a secret smile.

With the flowers arranged, the pink strawberry milkshake poured into long fluted glasses and her house twinkling with tidiness, Felicity finally sat down on her sofa.

She opened the letter again and, with a beaming smile, read through it one more time. Suddenly the doorbell rang and Felicity hastily stuffed it into a drawer.

✶ ✶ ✶

"Hello!" sang Felicity to her friends, bouncing up and down with delight in the doorway.

Holly, Polly and Daisy stared strangely at their friend.

"Have you been eating too many sweets again, Felicity?" asked Polly concerned.

"No, but I have some really exciting news. I've been desperate to tell you all week but with one thing and another the week has just flown by and this is the first chance I've had time to speak to you properly. This is going to be the best day ever!"

"It will be the best day ever, once we've given you your surprise," said Holly, grinning secretively and holding out a cake box.

"A chocolate cake, from The Sticky Bun, how FANTASTIC!" exclaimed Felicity.

"Open it, then," said Polly, who couldn't bear to wait any longer. She nudged the chocolate cake box towards Felicity.

Holly, Polly and Daisy held their breath with excitement as Felicity slowly opened the lid to reveal a scrumptious chocolate cake. Wafer-thin layers of chocolate balanced delicately on thick cream, freckled with tiny strawberries. Perfect!

"Thank you – I love it! Now, I must give you my surprise!" said Felicity as she sliced the cake into fairy bite-sized pieces.

Then she saw the pink envelope

hidden underneath the cake. "A card too! Oh thank you!" she said picking it up and starting to open it. "Anyway, my news! You're never going to believe this, but I'm finally going to meet Bea! In real life! She's invited me to stay with her at half-term."

Felicity was so busy slicing the cake that she didn't see her friends' wings droop and their excited faces turn to disappointment.

"And there's even more good news…" said Felicity, stopping in her tracks as she took the card from the pink envelope and looked at it. "This looks just like a scene from Petal Mountain."

"It is a scene from Petal Mountain!" said Polly quietly.

And as Felicity opened the card to read what was inside a pink ticket for a holiday at half-term fluttered to the table.

"I don't believe it!" said Felicity "What... how...?"

"We thought we could spend some fairy fun time together somewhere nice on holiday, so we booked for us all to go to Petal Mountain," Holly explained. "But it looks as if we've been beaten to it."

"But that was what I wanted to tell you today!" Felicity said. "I was telling Bea all about you when I realised that you would get on brilliantly with Bea's friends! Daisy, she has a friend called Jasmine who loves flowers and would love you. Polly, Bea's friend Amber wants to be a tooth fairy like you, and Holly, Star loves the latest fashion trends just like you!"

Felicity paused for breath and smiled at her friends' stunned faces.

"So we decided to surprise you with a holiday to visit Bea's friends. That's why I've been so busy over the last few weeks – I've been planning a holiday for you."

"But Felicity how can we visit Bea's friends if we will be on holiday in Petal Mountain?" asked Daisy still confused.

"That's the best thing about it – they live in Petal Mountain!" Felicity answered, starting to jump up and down with excitement as her friend's confused expressions turned to delight. "I thought I'd told you all where Bea lives but I must have forgotten!"

"So we can still go to Petal Mountain?" asked Daisy starting to jump up and down too.

"And we're going to meet Bea and all her friends too?" asked Holly jumping higher and higher.

"Yes! And just think of the new friends we're all going to make!" said Felicity nearly touching the roof.

"We'd better get planning, then," suggested Polly, pulling out Petal Mountain Travel Guide from her bag. "There's so much to see and do there and only a week to do it in!"

Gather friends
like flowers

to make a beautiful
bouquet

Magical Medicine

Felicity Wishes and her fairy friends were going on holiday together to visit Bea, Felicity's new penfriend, and her best friends in Petal Mountain. Morning, noon and night, all the fairies talked about and thought about was their holiday.

It was double history and Felicity was finding it hard to concentrate on her textbook – Fairy World, Part four. Instead of listing who did what when, Felicity was busy scribbling down a list of why she was such a lucky fairy!

MY LUCKY LIST
by Felicity Wishes

1. I am going on holiday.

2. I am going somewhere I had only dreamt about going before now.

3. I get to meet my new penfriend for the first time.

4. All my best friends are coming too.

5. My penfriend gets to meet...

"FELICITY!" shouted Miss Fossil at the front of the class. "PAY ATTENTION!"

30

"Sorry, Miss Fossil," replied Felicity sheepishly as she quickly hid her list under the desk.

She could hardly wait for the class, and the day, to be over. Every morning before she got dressed Felicity had been crossing off the days, and in class she'd even been crossing off the minutes.

"I feel terrible wishing my days away like this," said Felicity to Polly on their way to Sparkles café. "I just can't wait. Seven days, seventeen hours and..." she checked her watch, "thirty-two minutes!"

"Oh Felicity!" said Polly giggling. "It'll be here before you know it."

* * *

Felicity and Polly had arranged to meet Daisy and Holly at Sparkles to make their final holiday arrangements. There was still so much to do, and time was running out.

"Right," said Polly taking charge and bringing out her checklist.

"Oh, before we start," Felicity interrupted, "I've got something for you all!"

And from her bag Felicity pulled out a large yellow envelope in a cloud of glitter. Holly, Polly and Daisy had seen these envelopes before.

"It's one of your letters from your penfriend Bea, isn't it?" asked Polly.

"Not my letter," said Felicity "your letter!"

Holly, Polly and Daisy looked confused.

"Open it!" urged Felicity excitedly handing it over.

Holly quickly tore open the envelope as the others peered over her shoulder to read it.

"It's a map! And there's a note," said Holly curiously.

Dear Holly, Polly and Daisy,

Felicity has told me so much about you. And I'm sure she's told you all about my best friends — Amber, Star and Jasmine. We're all really looking forward to meeting you and I know the eight of us are going to have so much fun together! I've drawn a map of Petal Mountain and marked on it all the exciting things we can do or see. There won't be enough time to do them all, so let me know which ones you like the sound of most and I will book tickets.

Sparkly wishes,

Bea x x x

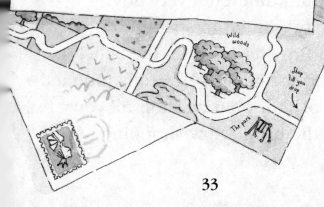

"That's really nice of her," said Polly excitedly. "And her friends sound so lovely."

"And she put one kiss for each of us," said Daisy analysing the letter, "which is an extra sign of niceness." Holly opened the map and spread it out on the table.

"Wow!" chorused the fairies. "There are so many things to do!"

"I think I'll put my checklist away until tomorrow!" said Polly more excited about the map.

* * *

By the time they left Sparkles, the fairy friends had decided on an itinerary that was fun-filled with something different every day.

Felicity wanted to spend a day at Ocean Bay, relaxing on the beach in the warm summer sun. Holly planned a day of shopping at Shop til' you Drop, the brand new shopping complex. Daisy was keen to visit the Petal Project to check out the latest fairy-made flowers. And Polly insisted on visiting the local museum as she sensibly felt that they all needed to do something educational on their trip.

"This trip is going to be the best," Felicity shouted after her friends as she waved goodbye outside the café.

"The best holiday ever," agreed Daisy excitedly.

* * *

When Felicity arrived home, she counted the days to go on her calendar and made herself a super-frothy strawberry smoothie.

She picked up today's edition of The Daily Flutter

and flicked through the pages until she came to the weather section.

"Yippee!" she cheered out loud when she saw that the weather was going to be hot and sunny in Petal Mountain. "At last I can wear my new pink swimsuit!" she thought.

But then Felicity noticed something else that made her frown. It was also the rainy season in Petal Mountain and thunderstorms were possible daily.

"Oh no!" Felicity gasped, "What am I going to tell the others?"

After much thought, Felicity decided not to tell the others the last part of the weather report as it may not rain and she didn't want to spoil their excitement.

* * *

The weekend soon came and the fairies met on the corner of the High Street to get all the lovely things

they needed for their holiday.

"We have lots to do and get today and only an afternoon to do it in so I've planned a schedule for the day," said Polly, pulling out a list from her bag.

"Not another list," sighed Holly.

Felicity and Daisy struggled to contain their giggles. Polly was always making lists for everything.

"If we don't follow my list today, we may end up on holiday without some vital things – can you imagine if you forgot to buy your favourite lipgloss, Holly?"

"Hmm, I see what you mean," said Holly. "Where to first then?"

And with that, the fairies headed straight to Star Treatment for their holiday beauty treatments. Holly had a facial, Felicity had a wing massage, Daisy had a hand treatment and Polly had a nice long foot soak.

They had heard that the fairies from Petal Mountain were very beautiful so they wanted to look their best for their trip.

* * *

With glowing faces, relaxed wings, soft hands and twinkling feet, the fairies fluttered to the next place on Polly's list – Fairy Mart.

The fairies had never been anywhere exotic before and weren't sure whether they would be able to get all their favourite treats there so they decided to stock up on a few things before they left!

With bags full of Twinkle Bars, Toffee Apples, Raspberry Laces and Cheesy Puffs, the fairies staggered out of the shop.

"At least we won't starve if we don't like the food in Petal Mountain," giggled Daisy as she looked at all their bags.

"Where to next?" asked Felicity.

"The most important place of all – Top Fairy – they have just had their latest delivery of summer clothes in!" said Polly, finding it hard to contain her excitement.

✳ ✳ ✳

The fairies gasped when they entered Top Fairy – there were rows and rows of red tops, yellow skirts, pink cardigans, green dresses, orange coats, purple wings and blue crowns – just like a rainbow!

TOP FAIRY BAGS AND SHO

Changing rooms

"I'm in heaven!" exclaimed Holly as she started to work her way through the racks of clothes.

"Don't forget, there's only so much you can fit in your suitcase," said Polly sensibly to the fairies.

Felicity, Holly and Daisy ignored Polly's advice and headed straight to the changing rooms with arms full of clothes.

As the fairies were leaving the shop with their summer selection, Felicity noticed a rail of raincoats in the corner of the room. For a brief second, Felicity considered suggesting that they get a raincoat but decided that positive thinking was the best option as it might not rain after all.

✳ ✳ ✳

As soon as Felicity arrived home, she started to pack, but unfortunately packing wasn't as straightforward as she had expected. Felicity was sure that she hadn't bought that many things but her suitcase wouldn't close.

"If only I could use a little fairy magic to close this case," sighed Felicity, knowing that she would never dare make a wish for her own gain. It was against the fairy law.

After a frustrating evening of trying to pack her case, Felicity phoned Polly to ask for her help. Polly always knew what to do in tricky situations.

"Felicity!" Polly exclaimed as she found her sitting on her suitcase, desperately trying to close it. "What have you got in there?"

"Only a few essential items," said Felicity telling a tiny white lie.

Polly opened Felicity's case and jumped back to avoid the piles of sweets and chocolates that fell onto the floor.

"But Felicity, you've hardly got any clothes in here!" she said, rummaging through. "It's all sweets! You're going to have to leave some of them behind."

Felicity agreed reluctantly and together they decided which sweets she was going to leave behind. When they had re-packed the bag, it did close this time, but only with Felicity and Daisy both sitting on the top of it!

* * *

At last, Felicity was all set for her holiday. It was only when she stood sleepy-eyed in front of her calendar that night that she realised she had one more thing to do before she went away. The words 'Dr Goodness 4.20pm' stood out in large pink letters. Felicity gulped.

Petal Mountain was on the opposite side of Fairy World – everything was different there; the water, the air, the food, even the language had funny words. To stop them from getting poorly from anything they weren't used to, each of the fairies had to have three types of medicine before they went.

Felicity had rather enjoyed the sugar lump she'd had on her first visit three weeks ago.

The spoonful of medicine Dr Goodness had given her on her second visit had been much less yummy, in fact it was horrid, and now she was worried what was in store for her on this third and final visit.

"What if it's a jab?" whispered Felicity to Polly in assembly.

"No! Worst than that what if it's a jab in your bottom!" giggled Holly.

"Well, at least we are all going together," said Daisy. "We can hold each other's hands and tell funny stories to each other to keep our minds off it."

* * *

For the first time in weeks Felicity wanted the minutes to last longer in class. She was getting more and more nervous about what awaited her at the doctors.

"I'm scared," said Felicity to Daisy fretting.

"Don't be scared, it'll be fine, I'm sure," said Daisy, trying to reassure herself as much as Felicity.

"If you two have something to say perhaps you would like to share it with the whole class," said Miss Meandering.

Holly and Felicity shook their heads.

"Good, now if everyone can turn to page fifty-seven, we'll start reading the section marked 'Mountains'."

Felicity wished she could concentrate more on the class, she was dying to know all about where her penfriend lived, and where, soon, her and all her friends would be going on holiday. But again and again her mind kept drifting to horrible visions of her visit to the doctors.

In what seemed like no time, the

lesson was over. Felicity, Holly, Polly and Daisy packed away their books reluctantly and slowly made their way to see Dr Goodness at the school medical centre.

"Dr Goodness will see you now," said the slight receptionist over the top of her glasses.

Felicity's wings quivered and as she stood up her legs trembled. All the time she tried to keep thinking of the holiday.

"Is it OK if my friends keep me company?" she asked.

"That's fine," the receptionist said, smiling warmly at Felicity and her friends all holding hands.

Dr Goodness looked over her glasses as the four fairies walked in.

"Please do take a seat," she gestured to the chairs next to her. "Now, which one of you is Felicity Wishes?"

"Me," replied Felicity in a small voice. "And these are my friends, Holly, Polly and Daisy."

"Hello!" the fairies chorused quietly. They too were feeling a little nervous now.

"Ahh, I'm sure I've heard those names before... now, didn't you fairies have something to do with the school newspaper last term?"

"That's right," said Felicity and started telling Dr Goodness all about the exciting stories the fairies had uncovered.

She was so engrossed in telling her stories that Felicity didn't notice Dr Goodness showering her with precisely 30mg of Magical Protection Dust.

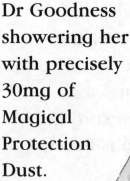

Felicity was literally out of breath when she'd finished telling the doctor all about their adventures.

"That all sounds great," remarked Dr Goodness. "Right, who's next?"

Felicity stared at the doctor, confused. "But don't you have to give me a jab?" she asked hesitantly.

"No, your final treatment was the Magical Protection Dust," Dr Goodness laughed. "And I just gave it to you!"

"You were so busy chatting that you didn't even notice it," giggled Daisy.

Felicity gave a large sigh of relief and then burst out laughing too!

* * *

After a long day, Felicity said goodbye to her friends and headed straight home and straight upstairs to her warm, cosy bed.

"Fancy worrying so much about the

doctor's appointment!" she laughed to herself as she snuggled down under her duvet. "But thank goodness it's over – now I really am set for our holiday!"

Holiday Check List

Camera ✓
Travel Guide ✓
Tickets ✓
Toothbrush ✓
Bikini ✓
3 x Wings: smart wings practical wings water wings ✓
Shoes ✓
Bags ✓
Dresses ✓
Undies ✓
Make-up ✓
Sun-tan cream ✓

Remembering the good things

will give you strength
to face the
bad things

Enchanted Escape

Felicity Wishes and her friends,
Holly, Polly and Daisy, were on their
way to the holiday of their dreams.
They were flying higher than any of
them had been before. The view was
amazing – fluffy white clouds lay like
a blanket of snow around the plane,
and a brilliant rainbow of pretty
pinks and lovely lilacs spread across
the sky.

None of the fairies had ever been
on a plane before and their trip from

Bloomfield International Airport to Petal Mountain would take a long seventeen hours. The fairies chatted excitedly about their holiday well into the night but eventually Polly sensibly decided that they should try and get some sleep. Once the friends had washed their faces, brushed their teeth and put on some comfortable clothes, the hostess turned off the lights. After the day's excitement, the fairies were exhausted so it wasn't long before they were all sound asleep.

* * *

"Look there she is!" said Felicity dropping her bag and running towards a small fairy waiting at the entrance to Petal Mountain.

"Bea!" cried Felicity hugging her. "You look just like your photo! I was worried I wouldn't recognise you!"

Bea was delighted to see Felicity

too. "I'm so happy you came, and with all your lovely friends."

"Come and meet them!" Felicity urged as she grabbed Bea's hand and fluttered over to Holly, Polly and Daisy who had collapsed in a heap on top of their cases.

Bea knew that Felicity and her friends would be tired after their long journey so had kindly organised for a bus to collect them and take them to their hotel. The fairies chatted excitedly non-stop all the way.

"Look at the stunning countryside!"
said Daisy opening the doors onto
their veranda when they checked into
their room. "It's not a bit like home –
there are flowers everywhere! I can't
wait to explore Petal Mountain
properly."

"And the fashion!" said Holly,
laughing as she hung over the rail
and pointed to a fairy with
three sets of wings.

"Imagine if we wore that in Little Blossoming!"

"Yum, and look at the food!" said Polly, who had picked up a purple spiky fruit from the bowl on the table and was sniffing it. "It smells like strawberries and melons together!"

"And don't forget the friends!" said Felicity. "What amazing new friends we'll have by the time we leave. Bea has invited us all to go to her house for tea so we can meet everyone and go through what we want to do. It is all so exciting!"

✳ ✳ ✳

Bea's house wasn't like any house the fairies had ever seen before. Set in a valley at the foot of Petal Mountain it appeared to hover just above the ground.

"Is it on stilts?" said Holly, squinting as they came up the path.

"No, I don't think it is," said Polly in disbelief. "I think it's floating!"

"How are we going to ring the bell?" asked Felicity, looking up at the front door from the ground.

"Fly!" said Polly, fluttering her wings and giggling. "Sometimes in Little Blossoming it's easy to forget you're a fairy, but here it seems as though that's what it's all about."

"I know what you mean," said Felicity. "There's definitely something very special about this place."

As she pulled on the large golden chain, all four fairies found themselves whisked up in a cloud of glitter and transported into Bea's hallway.

"Hello!" said Bea flying towards them.

"There's no floor!" said Felicity, panicking.

"Hardly any of the houses here have floors, although most hotels do because it's what the tourists are used to, but we prefer wing power to walking."

"What do you do when your wings get tired?" said Polly, already feeling the strain.

"Oh, we've got chairs and beds and things!" said Bea laughing. "We're not that strange! Come through to the sitting room and you can meet the others."

∗ ∗ ∗

It was all very strange to Felicity, Holly, Polly and Daisy. All the furniture looked similar but instead of resting on the ground it was suspended from the ceiling with fine threads of sparkly gold.

"These are my friends - Jasmine, Amber and Star," said Bea, gesturing to the other fairies in the room.

Felicity ran up to Bea's friends and gave them the biggest squeeze possible. Bea's friends looked a little overwhelmed at first but soon realised that Felicity was just being friendly.

Holly, Polly and Daisy in turn introduced themselves to Bea's friends.

"Sit down and have a chat and I'll get you all something to drink," Bea offered, fluttering out of the room.

✳ ✳ ✳

A little shy at first, the fairy friends found conversation awkward, but by the time Bea had returned with the drinks Holly and Star were busy talking about the latest catwalk trends. Daisy and Jasmine were engrossed in the latest edition of Magic Gardens, and Polly and Amber were swapping studying techniques. Felicity beamed when Bea came into the room – it was lovely to see their friends getting on so well.

"I've made everyone a special fruit cocktail – 'Friendship Fizz'," said Bea, handing out tall glasses filled with the juices of exotic fruits.

"I'd like to make a toast," said Felicity blushing slightly at the attention. "Here's to a happy holiday!" And everyone raised their glasses and cheered.

* * *

By the time Felicity and her friends left

Bea's house, their holiday plans were sorted. Bea had organised trips to see everything they had put on their wish list. But tomorrow it was Daisy's special day and Bea had organised a trip to the top of Petal Mountain to see some of the rare species of flowers.

"I hope we don't have to fly there as my wings still ache," said Daisy as she took them off and hung them over the back of the hotel chair.

"Mine are so tired I haven't the energy to take them off," said Felicity snuggling under the duvet with her wings on!

"I've suddenly realised that wearing three pairs of wings may be more about being practical than being fashionable!" said Holly thoughtfully as the fairies started to fall into a deep, cosy sleep.

* * *

When all the fairies met up the next day Felicity and her friends were still finding it hard to adjust to the differences.

"We had chocolate cake for breakfast!" said Polly to Amber shocked. "Is that normal round here?"

"No, it's probably just because you're in a hotel," said Amber.

Polly looked relieved. One day she hoped to be a tooth fairy and sweet things she believed should always be eaten in moderation, and certainly not for breakfast!

"Mostly we just have Sugar Cloudberry Gateau at home for breakfast," said Amber casually.

Polly gulped.

"Everyone ready?" said Bea, taking charge and looping arms with Felicity.

Holly checked over her shoulder to make sure her new pair of triple wings were flapping in time. She and Star had slipped out to the shops first thing to find a very classy-looking set of triple wings to match Holly's new holiday dress.

"Ready when you are!" they all replied enthusiastically.

"Right," continued Bea, "the most important thing to do is stick together. Parts of the path are very overgrown which makes it difficult to see where you're supposed to be flying. Follow me!"

* * *

The fairy friends flew in single file under the large silver arch that crowned the entrance to the base of the mountain. After handing in their tickets each fairy was given a map. The view from the bottom of the mountain was incredible - the whole mountain appeared to be made up of tiny rainbow petals that merged to

make it glow. The wonderful fresh
smell of exotic flowers filled the air
and with each breath the fairies took,
they felt lighter and lighter until
it was almost as if they were
floating to the top of
the mountain.

WELCOME TO PETAL MOUNTAIN

"Oh my wing's snagged," said Holly, suddenly feeling a tug from behind and looking back to see the fabric unravel behind her.

"Don't worry," said Bea who'd climbed the mountain before, "the fresh mountain air lifts you so that you barely have to flap."

Daisy was in raptures. Not only had she seen flowers she'd never dreamed even existed before, she'd found a soul mate in Jasmine who's speciality was seeds. When Jasmine left school, she wanted to be a Nature Fairy, collecting, planting and nurturing seeds until they became strong plants.

Anxious to see more and more, Daisy and Jasmine had found themselves at the front of the group.

"Look over there!" cried Daisy, putting her hand over her mouth in astonishment. "What's that?!" she said pointing to a beautiful pink flower that towered over the fairies.

Jasmine was silent for a few moments.

"It's a Sweet Saffire," she finally said. "They are quite rare around here. Let's take a closer look."

The fairies had to fly carefully through large green leaves and sticky stems before they reached the enormous billowing petals that waved like huge sails in the wind.

Soon all the fairy friends were standing in awe.

"I've never seen anything like it," said Felicity. "There are so many things you have that are strange to us.

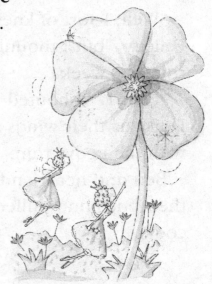

I don't know what to find odd and
what not to any more!"

* * *

Suddenly there was a low, deep
rumble overhead. Felicity and her
friends froze mid-air.

"Don't worry it's only a thunderstorm
coming," said Bea casually.

"A thunderstorm!" wailed Holly, Polly
and Daisy.

"Surely you knew that it was the
rainy season here?" asked Bea as the
skies opened and the rain started to
pour heavier and heavier.

"Well, I sort of knew," confessed
Felicity, "but I thought it might not
rain this week."

"Felicity!" shouted Holly, Polly and
Daisy as their wings started to droop
with the heavy rain.

Bea and her friends reached into
their bags and pulled out their rain
coats.

"Have you not brought any rain coats?" asked Jasmine.

"No, sorry," said Felicity looking down at the ground so that she didn't see her friends' distraught faces.

"Well, it's a good job we brought spare ones, isn't it?" giggled Star as she pulled out four more rain coats.

"Hooray!" Felicity, Holly, Polly and Daisy cheered as they quickly put on their coats and continued on their journey to the top of the mountain.

✳ ✳ ✳

The view from the top was breath-taking! Everyone was speechless and sat quietly admiring the view.

"It'll be dark soon," said Bea after she realised they'd been there for over an hour. "We had better head back."

Suddenly she went pale.

"Does anyone remember the way?" said Bea looking round anxiously.

"Um, no," said Felicity spinning round and round on the spot.

"I don't want to alarm anyone but I think we're lost!"

"Oh goodness," said Daisy.

"Don't worry, I'm sure it will be fine," said Polly getting out her map. "It's not dark yet and we can still see our way."

"Not dark yet!" said Holly panicking, looking up at the sky that was getting blacker by the minute. What are we going to do?! I don't want to spend the rest of my holiday on a mountain."

"They'll be no need," urged Polly. "Look, I think we're just about… here…"

Bea took a look at the map.

"No, we passed that point a while ago. We might be somewhere around here…"

"Oh this is a disaster!" wailed Holly dramatically.

Holly slumped down in despair or rather tried to slump down but her wing snagged again on a flower stem.

"Typical," she said as she buried her head in her hands ready to give up.

Felicity bent down to give her friend a hug and as she did her arm got tangled in the threads from Holly's torn wing. Slowly a huge beaming smile spread across Felicity's face.

"You can show us the way home Holly!" announced Felicity.

"Ha-ha," said Holly sulking.

"No really!" said Felicity, "Look!"

And all the fairies cheered as they saw that the silk thread from Holly's broken wing led a trail right back to where their journey had begun.

* * *

When the fairies finally got back to their hotel, they collapsed in a heap on the bed.

"Well I think that's enough excitement for one day," said Felicity.

"I think it's enough excitement for one holiday," said Holly. "I vote we spend the rest of our time away safely on the beach."

"Me too!" chorused Felicity, Polly and Daisy.

* * *

After six whole days on the beach playing in the warm summer sun, swimming in the cool water and eating lots of yummy tropical food, the fairies finally had to wave goodbye to their new friends.

As the fairies were leaving, Holly hugged Star, Polly hugged Amber, Daisy hugged Jasmine, and a tearful Felicity gave Bea the biggest hug of all.

"I'm really going to miss you," weeped Felicity, "but best friends always stick together and we will be friends forever."

"I'll miss you too Felicity," said Bea with a lump in her throat.

"We'll write to each other every week and you and your friends must come and stay with us next holiday," pleaded Felicity.

"We would love to, thank you," said Bea speaking on behalf of her friends.

"And we'll come and stay again," said Daisy. "There's still so much we haven't seen."

"As long as we don't visit any more mountains, I'll be there!" said Holly giggling.

Look with magic in your heart

and the way forward will
be revealed

If you enjoyed this book, why not try another of these fantastic story collections?

Clutter Clean-out

Designer Drama

Newspaper Nerves

Star Surprise

Enchanted Escape

Friends Forever

Sensational Secrets

Whispering Wishes

Also available in the Felicity Wishes range:

Felicity Wishes: Secrets and Surprises

Felicity Wishes is planning her birthday party but it seems none of her friends can come. Will Felicity end up celebrating her birthday alone?

Felicity Wishes: Snowflakes and Sparkledust

It is time for spring to arrive in Little Blossoming but there is a problem and winter is staying put. Can Felicity Wishes get the seasons back on track?